EDGES

Chase or Die

Book 9

Bjorn Esterday Was Not Born Yesterday

Wynter Sommers

GJ dePillis

Published by Pure Force Enterprises, Inc.
California, USA
Since 2002

ISBN-13: 978-1-7184-0010-8
ISBN-10: 1-7184-0010-1

DEDICATION

To all of us whose hearts reach out to change the world around, whose minds calculate the next strategic move, whose souls crave adventure and value the freedoms of democracy. To the spirit harnessing the power of fiction to alter our reality, making the world a better place for everyone.

Bjorn Esterday Was Not Born Yesterday Series

Firebrand (9 Stories +Conversation Station Book)
Edges (9 Stories +Conversation Station Book)
Gone (18 Stories + 2 Conversation Station Books)

Bjorn EDGES Series
EDGES Book 1-Swift Encounter
EDGES Book 2-Rousing Attack
EDGES Book 3-One Foot Under
EDGES Book 4-Earthshake
EDGES Book 5-Broken String
EDGES Book 6-Key Witness
EDGES Book 7-Who is She?
EDGES Book 8-Vanish
EDGES Book 9-Chase or Die

Bjorn Series Alternate Reading Plan

1st   Edges Book 1
2nd Edges Book 2
3rd   Gone Book 1
4th   Firebrand Book 1
5th   Edges Book 3
6th   Firebrand Book 2
7th   Gone Book 2
8th   Gone Book 3
9th   Firebrand Book 3
10th Gone Book 4
11th Firebrand Book 4
12th Gone Book 5
13th Gone Book 6
14th Edges Book 4
15th Firebrand Book 5
16th Gone Book 7
17th Firebrand Book 6
18th Gone Book 8
19th Firebrand Book 7
20th Gone Book 9
21st Firebrand Book 8
22nd Gone Book 10
23rd Gone Book 11
24th Gone Book 12
25th Gone Book 13
26th Firebrand Book 9 (End)
27th Gone Book 14
28th Gone Book 15
29th Gone Book 16
30th Gone Book 17
31st Gone Book 18 (End)
32nd Edges Book 5
33rd Edges Book 6
34th Edges Book 7
35th Edges Book 8
36th Edges Book 9 (End)

CONTENTS

ACKNOWLEDGMENTS

To all those gentle souls who have graciously given tokens of love, hope, and kind considerations to others.

0 Preface

We discover that although Pip is greedy, he is sure he did not murder his father, Skipper Courtly.

Pip just wants money and needs help to get out of jail. He does. However, he is double crossed. But by whom?

The driverless car, which follows Bjorn earlier, now strikes and nearly kills all the suspects crowded together in front of the SP station. This attack also provides a distraction, allowing Pip to escape with a cohort.

Bjorn follows Pip and tries to discover who Pip's partner is. In the process, Bjorn is knocked out and locked up.

i

Later, he wakens, only to see that he is caged, and about to be killed. Suspended from a high ceiling, he hears a timer running out which will release Bjorn to fall into a vat of deadly acid, and be conveniently "recycled". Who set him up?

1 CHAPTER Year 2036: Balloons, Balloons (Continuous Ch 85)

The truck sputtered to a stop outside the expansive fairgrounds. Its battery was spent. Empty. Dead. Bjorn, glad the truck had lasted this long before giving out, jumped down from the cab and shoved his way through the huge crowd.

He was trying to catch the last light of the evening, frantically searching for the man responsible for orchestrating the largest white-collar theft in the city's history.

A man guilty of murder.

A man about to get away free.

Everyone in the immense mass of celebrants was focused on the festivities at hand. Already, huge balloons were slowly rising, drifting up into the air, dotting the dusky sky.

Hundreds of spectators were out for the sunset candlelight hot air balloon celebration in the open field.

This event had started years earlier when small satellites were attached to balloons and floated up into the stratosphere to create a better network of communication.

Even though, that function had become antiquated, the moonlight balloon ride was still an event that brought all the people out to celebrate.

One by one, each hot air balloon, brightly colored, and decorated with streamers, signs, and sparkling lights were launched impressively into the night sky.

Photographers and spectators waited

on the ground as each balloon rose slowly to join the others, transforming the inky evening canvas into a dramatic mystical brilliant display.

Bjorn knew that every bit of Courtly money would now go to this man if the hospital staff couldn't keep Pip alive. Bjorn's target didn't realize that there was still one more Courtly who could claim the inheritance.

Alexandra.

If he found out about her, she could count her life in days. Now, the killer, who assumed he had perfected his efforts with absolute success, planned an escape that would take him far away without even a credit trail.

Bjorn understood what the castle Foreman had meant. The Foreman just wanted to find Skipper to get that memo signed, and didn't realize he had interrupted the murderer's plan to drown Sarah. Frustrated, the murderer went on to kill Skip, attack Pip, and even tried to get rid of Sarah and Bjorn himself.

Bjorn didn't have time to berate himself for not seeing the pattern until now.

He barely had time to breathe as he pushed through the drunken crowd which was already wreathed in a drug blurred haze.

Searching, Bjorn zeroed in on only the men. He turned one around by the shoulder, but it was the wrong man. Again, another one. Wrong. Again. Wrong. Hastily apologetic, Bjorn strode away, ignoring the mutterings of how rude he was.

Raucous attendees seemed to multiply before him. The crowds made it more and more difficult for Bjorn to weave his way between the baskets as he tried to search for that man. Their laughing and giggling contrasted with Bjorn's intense focus. He had to find his quarry in time before the monster really did float away without a trace.

Stranger after stranger. One after the next. Man after man. Bjorn felt he was close, but was frustrated that each man he thought he recognized, turned out to be another error.

The hot air balloons majestically floated up and away into the clear night, one by one, as they were released.

Then, Bjorn targeted one particular basket. The man was alone, his balloon already lifting off.

Bjorn moved quickly. The man had his back turned, busying himself with launch procedures. Bjorn hesitated. Is he making another mistake?

The man turned and saw Bjorn. Surprise froze him momentarily. Then his face twisted into a mask of rage.

Bjorn, in spite of himself, stared. Shocked. He couldn't believe his eyes! It was this man! This man! This very man! All along!

This mild mannered... Always pleasant... kindly... friendly... The ever-helpful... Attorney Atsushi!

Attorney Atsushi!

Attorney Atsushi had, in fact, always

been the master-mind, the coldly murderous beast, behind all these deadly machinations!

Bjorn charged the rising balloon, heaved himself into the basket, making it sway as it began to ascend. It wobbled with the sudden jolt of weight being added to it, causing the balloon to shift off course, heading toward a dirt road encircling the parked balloon baskets.

"You will not jeopardize a plan I've crafted for the last seven years, Mr. Esterday," Atsushi spat.

The un-partitioned 42 by 72 inch basket tipped, throwing Bjorn off balance and into Atsushi. Atsushi broke free, regained his footing and grabbed a rough coil of rope at his feet to lash out at Bjorn.

Bjorn fell back, his knee buckled, and he hit his head on the edge of the basket.

Atsushi blurted as he began to unwind the heavy rope with gloved hands, "I could have killed Skipper with a gun, the weapon of choice for idiots and morons,"

Atsushi shouted as the wind whipped away his words. "Instead," Atshsui spat, "I chose diversion and misdirection. The champagne I gave Pip has finally finished him off, and you will be yesterday's news, Mr. Esterday."

By now, the balloon had wafted six stories up into the air.

As Bjorn struggled to his feet, Atsushi pulled up his sleeve to reveal a small drone control on his wrist. He gave it a tap which summoned a driverless vehicle to appear beneath them, following their movements from the ground.

Bjorn looked over the edge. Crowds were cheering as hundreds of balloons filled the air, lit by the setting sun just sinking behind the horizon.

Bjorn noted the drone below Atsushi's basket was identical to the vehicle which had plowed into them at the SP station. Bjorn realized Atsushi had created that diversion also.

It suddenly occurred to Bjorn that he really could die if he fell out. He was determined to survive.

"You can't kill me with all these witnesses around," Bjorn shouted as he maneuvered away from Atsushi.

"If I had a gun," Atsushi countered, "I could shoot you in the face right now in front of everybody. If you survived, you'd be apologizing to me for stepping into my line of fire. Don't you get it? It doesn't matter, anymore."

The wind gusted roughly, swaying the basket, keeping both men off balance.

Bjorn said, with one hand on a roll bar, trying to keep from slipping, "What doesn't matter? Anything? Nothing?"

Bjorn thought of Sarah... this man had almost succeeded... the pain of that memory choked Bjorn...

With a kick, Atsushi pushed Bjorn back, then grabbed the rope. Atsushi tapped his wrist-sized control and the rope anchor locked.

Atsushi sneered, "Nothing personal. Drowning Sarah would have stopped her from sharing those incriminating papers. She escaped. She was the first I tried to kill. I learned from my mistakes. So, then I hired an actor to verify there were no other copies. But now it doesn't matter if she lives or dies. I own everything!"

"You fabricated the legend of the ghost? To drown Skipper!" Bjorn shouted.

"Yes. But I got him, anyway!" screamed Atsushi, eager to boast in safety to the man about to die. "With Mayfounder gas! By using skills from Pip's glass-blowing classes. And even better, that little naïve Earthie got his fingerprints all over Skipper's violin, implicating him, as well. Look here! Look there! Suspects abound! But suspicion will never touch me. I am precious and separate! All because now I own everything! Money! Money! All of it mine!"

"Sound as nutty as you want, Atsushi... No judge will buy it. The law will catch up with you," Bjorn muttered, as he searched to see if he could grab the rope from Atsushi.

9

The balloon was spinning and dipping, buffeted by wild gusts of wind. Atsushi grabbed onto the basket edge to catch his balance.

"You still don't get it!" roared Atsushi. "Now that Pip has signed everything over to me, I am above the law. I can do anything I want. Even kill you. And they will worship me!"

Bjorn did not see Atsushi give an abrupt tug and unfurl a grip on the rope into which Atsushi slipped his two gloved hands.

Then, the bottom of the basket dropped away and Atsushi began a controlled slide down the rope to the awaiting vehicle below, which was keeping pace with the balloon.

The sudden displacement of weight caused the basket to lurch. Bjorn jumped for the silks, which ripped away in his hands.

Bjorn, grabbed onto the basket support bar as his feet scrambled in empty space. Atsushi had almost reached the vehicle below.

The top of the driverless car opened up, letting Atsushi drop in.

Ignoring howling blasts of wind around him, Bjorn leapt in mid-air to grab the rope Atsushi just used. Sliding bare-handed to follow after Atsushi, Bjorn felt his hands burn raw as the rough rope ate into the flesh of his palms.

Atsushi was busy tapping his wrist to release the rope.

About ten feet above the car, Bjorn felt the rope go limp and drop with him. Atsushi's remote command had released the rope's anchor and started to shut the top of the vehicle. As the roof was closing, Bjorn also fell in, landing right on top of Atsushi, just as Atsushi was looking up.

The wrist control Atsushi wore to navigate his drone, slammed into the window, causing the vehicle to abruptly change direction. Bjorn realized he had to get hold of the controls on Atsushi's forearm in order to stop the swerving vehicle.

11

As they struggled, Bjorn grabbed for one of the remotes on Atsushi's arm, causing the vehicle to suddenly spin around 180 degrees.

Bjorn clenched a fist and drove it straight into Atsushi's face. Atsushi's arm blocked the punch, but Bjorn's fist, landing on the controls again, forced the vehicle to squeal to an abrupt halt.

Panicked, Atsushi grabbed at another button and the vehicle leapt forward, throwing Bjorn into the back seat. With shaking hands, Atsushi fought G-forces as he grabbed his wrist again, sending the vehicle spinning in circles.

The crowds of people on the road raced in all directions trying to evade the vehicle's chaotic path.

Bjorn, with face pressed back from the centrifugal force, fought gravity to yank Atsushi's wrist and the vehicle took off sideways on two wheels, then flipped over onto its roof, opening all doors.

Both men fell out and lay motionless.

2 CHAPTER Year 2036: We Got It Covered (Continuous Ch 86)

Both men lay stunned on the ground.

Atsushi groaned as he stared up into the sky of lighted balloons. The sun had set, offsetting the twinkling balloons in a disorienting visual. Then, Atsushi saw the unconscious body of Bjorn sprawled motionless on the road two feet away from him. With a surge of adrenaline, he saw his chance to rid himself of this reporter.

Bjorn moved his head as he was just coming to.

Ignoring the gathering crowd, Atsushi lunged for his throat, choking Bjorn. Bjorn, disoriented and weak, tried to punch blindly, but Atsushi dodged, now fully focused on strangling Bjorn.

Behind Atsushi's head came the distinctive hum of a weapon charging up before firing. Atsushi instinctively froze.

"Think, then release," the stern voice of Detective Gene ordered.

Atsushi carefully loosened his fingers from around Bjorn's neck and slowly raised his hands. Then, Atsushi heard the harmonic whine of additional weapons readying to fire. Several red dots of light landed on the back of the kneeling Atsushi.

Cautiously, he turned around to see that Detective Gene was standing a few feet in front of a semi-circle of efficiently trained Soldier Police, all with weapons directly aimed at Atsushi.

Sammy Scribe burst through the crowd, followed by his Daily Memo team. They bounded right to where Atsushi was being arrested. The team machinery electronically recorded all action non-stop as Atsushi was restrained, then placed into a vehicle, and was finally driven away by Soldier Police.

Sammy leaned down to Bjorn, who was aching with his recent wounds. "Hey, Bjorn," Sammy grinned, "I got 'em here just in time."

"Yeah. Thanks, Sammy, for calling in that favor," Bjorn nodded wearily, "He confessed to all of it, but I didn't get it recorded. Not one word. I'm sorry."

"Hey!" Sammy smiled. "I called in the cavalry with Detective Gene. The gang, here, got hold of some new equipment. Targeted recording. We got visual and audio. It wasn't hard to spot the one balloon that was crazily swooping around up there. We figured that was you."

Bjorn gave a painful sigh of relief, "Maybe this story will convince the owners that we should have an Investigative Reporting division, again."

"Are you saying that you think the public is smarter than the owners give 'em credit for? That the people will demand truth, facts, and consequences for criminals?" Sammy laughed, "Who knows. Maybe. It's worth proposing it to them."

"I'm just glad to be alive," Bjorn said exhausted.

"Y'know, if your girlfriend hadn't convinced me that somebody was trying to frame Joshua Lantz for Skipper's murder...," Sammy shook his head, "I mean, Sarah figured out that Atsushi was the one who remotely drove that vehicle into us at the Station. You know, to throw suspicion off of himself. Because of her, the kid Joshua was released."

Medics moved in and began treating Bjorn for multiple injuries. Bjorn winced as one medic poured antiseptic over his palms, while the other cut lengths of bandaging to wrap around his hands.

Sammy continued, "The lab has Atsushi's aura pints on the vial and the violin, so it backs up your theory. I just wonder if Pip was in on it."

"He may have been at first," Bjorn surmised as he swallowed, his throat raw from shouting into the wind, "but Atsushi turned on Pip after he got his signature making Atsushi the new Courtly king," Bjorn explained. "By the way, where is Sarah?"

"Oh, she had something she needed to do. Said she may be gone a few days," Sammy replied evasively.

"A few days!" Bjorn rasped. "She never left word..."

"Said she tried to call you, but you didn't answer..." Sammy shrugged his shoulders as Bjorn was lifted into an ambulance.

Sammy added as he turned to walk away, "I gatta find a redmail station and get this footage processed. We got a story to run tomorrow."

Sammy smiled as he and the Daily Memo team hurried away.

3 CHAPTER   Year 2037: What? Who? Where? (Continuous Ch 87)

"What do you mean it's a surprise?" Bjorn asked.

"I mean you'll have to be patient. It's something I'm sure you'll love," Sarah winked at him as she helped him into his vehicle.

She tapped the auto-drive mode, setting a course to drive out of the city toward the Lantz farm. Bjorn's fingers extended from thin bandages which covered his almost-healed palms. He was just starting to use a crutch to get around.

18

"Well, I was going to tell you something, but I think I'll also keep it a surprise for later," Bjorn teased as the vehicle took off.

"Oh, don't be like that, Bjorn. Just tell me," Sarah urged as she tapped his arm cast. "Have you gotten more stubborn since they patched you up from your famous hot air balloon fall?"

"Nope. You've been with me for the last month and know everything that's happened, so I think I will keep something from you until later tonight. We will surprise each other at the right time," he said with a playful grin. "I probably already know your surprise, because you can't keep a secret. Especially not from me."

"I already surprised you," Sarah stated triumphantly, "by figuring out how to enter the latitude and longitude of the Lantz farm since your leg and arm are out of commission."

"Yes. That was a very helpful surprise." He kissed her on the cheek as the vehicle picked up speed.

19

"It was no easy task to figure out how to program the navigation component on this new fancy set of wheels you got to replace your old smashed-up vehicle," Sarah cooed.

"We'll see if your surprise is of the same caliber as my surprise," Bjorn teased.

"Challenge accepted, my dear." Sarah moved her hand to gently shake the fingers extending from his cast encased arm.

When they arrived, Bjorn, although hobbled by his injuries, leaned on his crutch as he tried to help Sarah out of the passenger side without falling over his own feet.

Young Joshua, seeing they had arrived, hurried on horseback to meet them.

"So pleased you were able to make it," said Joshua dismounting as he still held the reins. "Others will arrive later. Please, Miss Paradise, feel free to take this horse to ride back to the house. Alexandra will be happy to see you. It would be my pleasure to help guide Mr. Esterday along our rough path to our homestead."

Joshua handed the reins to Sarah.

"Oh, I don't mind staying with Bjorn, Joshua," Sarah offered.

"But, Alexandra did want to see you as soon as you arrived," Joshua urged.

"Go on, Sarah. Alexandra may want some girl-time," Bjorn encouraged.

"Well," Sarah said as Joshua helped her up into the stirrups, "Looks like fun! I haven't done this in a while." She swung her leg over the saddle, as her horse trotted off carrying Sarah toward the house.

Joshua turned to Bjorn. "I need to talk about what we discussed earlier."

Bjorn smiled, "You didn't propose yet?"

"No," Joshua reached down into his pocket and pulled out a pair of similar objects, except one was a small jar and the other a tiny box. "It's not our custom to give rings, but I went to the store you suggested and did purchase one. I want Alexandra to know that I respect the culture she comes from as she has always respected mine. But, I don't know how to present it to her. Would you please keep both this jar and box until the right time?"

"What is in which?" Bjorn asked.

"One is to give to Alexandra," Joshua clarified, "and the other is to give to Miss Paradise as a thank you for all she has done for us. My mother made these scented soaps especially for Miss Paradise. Women like gifts more than men. Jar of soap. Ring in box."

"Oh, okay," Bjorn agreed. He thought he would just be keeping Joshua's proposal a secret from Sarah, but now with this soap gift to Sarah, she would have two surprises.

Joshua said, "But the ring rattles around in that box."

Bjorn said, "I can fix that. Let's anchor it with a piece of string. Put it inside."

Bjorn pulled a thread from his jacket. It was just long enough to tie down the ring on the inside of the box.

Joshua smiled at the reporter's resourcefulness.

Joshua walked slowly, as Bjorn hobbled along with him. Joshua's parents saw them from afar and hurried to join them on the path toward their home. A few moments later, locals from the village, also headed down the winding path toward the Lantz homestead. The conversation became quite lively.

Joshua leaned toward Bjorn and muttered, "Remember, they'll be expecting me to have these, but you now have them. They make your pockets bulky, so you'll have to hide them someplace once we are inside. Don't tell me where you've put them until I'm ready. I'm too nervous."

Bjorn winked at Joshua, "Not a problem at all, my friend."

"Yes. Please keep them safe. I can't

risk her finding either one on me. I know I'm going to forget and mess this up."

"Use a rhyme as a mnemonic device. I saw an old movie once where a character used rhymes to remember what to do."

Meanwhile Sarah had dismounted from the horse and tethered its reins to the front post by the door. Alexandra opened the door, smiling, pleased to see her.

"Oh! Come in, Miss Paradise. Come in!" Alexandra was enthusiastic.

"I was happy when Joshua said he'd walk Bjorn back," Sarah explained as she followed Alexandra inside. "Alexandra, would you help me hide this. It's a surprise I've not given to Bjorn yet, and I thought tonight would be perfect."

"What is it, Miss Paradise?" Alexandra asked.

"It's a little paperweight in the shape of a harp. I picked it up at the music store. It's to let him know I think he's been an angel to me. Help me hide it, would you?" Sarah pleaded as she opened up her purse and brought out the tiny box.

"Let's put it someplace, now." Alexandra looked around. "I'll put it under the tarp over there." And she went to an alcove where some woodwork was covered by cloth.

"The tarp?" Sarah asked.

"Or I could place it behind the cask in the kitchen," Alexandra suggested as she moved Bjorn's gift.

"Oh, and later on, Alexandra," Sarah started, "Detective Gene may be stopping by, but don't tell Bjorn. That's also part of the surprise." Sarah smiled.

"It would be my pleasure to keep these confidences, Miss Paradise," Alexandra smiled. "Oh, I must tell you before Joshua and Mr. Esterday get here. Some of the women from our village have beautiful voices when they sing a-cappella. They should be arriving shortly."

"Will they sing tonight? Will Mr. and Mrs. Lantz be here, also?" Sarah asked.

"Of course, Miss Paradise. Yes to both questions," Alexandra beamed, suppressing a giggle.

Alexandra looked out the window. "They've met up with Mr. Esterday and Joshua on the path. Oh, and it looks as if some of the local women are arriving already with their husbands."

Alexandra scampered about filling cups with beverages to offer to the arriving clan.

When the small party came in, the room became effervescent with conversation.

Noah Lantz asked Bjorn, "If Attorney Atsushi was behind all this, why didn't Skipper or Pip Courtly suspect anything?"

Bjorn replied, "Don't know. Lust for power may have made Skipper Courtly compromise his values, so he and Pip were willing to look the other way when Atsushi manipulated the game."

Ruth chimed in, "Matthew six tells us

you cannot serve both God and money."

Noah added, "Timothy ten warns that the love of money is the root of all evil."

"Yeah," Bjorn said, "You can say that, again."

He hobbled over to a soft sturdy couch. Before his rear hit the seat, Joshua gave him a panicked look. Bjorn had shoved the two items that were given to him in his roomy pockets and one was about to slip out.

Quickly, Bjorn stood up again and stepped back toward an alcove of wood working covered by a tarp. Gingerly, he slipped one box under the tarp when nobody was looking and then hobbled back nonchalantly to the sofa. Then, he hid the other container nearby.

Noah Lantz sat on a wooden rocking chair and leaned in toward Bjorn to ask, "So what of this law that would make an employee, like my Joshua, an object that could be depreciated and then discarded?"

Across the room, the ladies gathered around Ruth, as she busily introduced them to Sarah.

The men settled in chairs and sat on the sofa around Noah and Bjorn.

Bjorn replied to Noah's question, "They have run into angry objections over the worker depreciation idea. It's not a law. They say it never will be. But keep alert to them. Let's hope they realize employees are people too, and should not be legally killed off by a corporate manager when 'fully deprecated'."

Sarah wandered over toward the wood working alcove, now forgetting if Alexandra had stowed her tiny harp under the thick covering or had she put it someplace else.

To herself she muttered, "The harp is under the tarp."

Bjorn, seeing Sarah getting too close to where he had just hidden Joshua's box called, "Sarah? What did you say?"

Startled, Sarah noticed the small group

staring at her, "Um. I was wondering if the carp was looking sharp."

"What is she speaking about?" Ruth leaned over to Bjorn.

Alexandra, realizing that Sarah had forgotten that Bjorn's gift-wrapped harp had been moved, said, "Miss Paradise, we won't be having carp for dinner. It would be too much of a... task."

Noah perplexed stated, "Carp is no task to prepare, child. You clean it, grill it..."

Sarah, understanding now that Alexandra meant "cask", moved away from the tarp covered wood working area and headed toward the kitchen. Alexandra intercepted her.

"Miss Paradise," Alexandra started, "I'd like to introduce you to our church a-cappella music group leader."

A short elderly lady stepped forward, holding a small baton. "We shall be delighted to sing the very moment you let us know."

Sarah smiled broadly, "Thank you. I

look forward to it."

Alexandra walked with Sarah toward the kitchen to whisper, "She's a little hard of hearing, but has excellent pitch."

Joshua and Bjorn gave each other a quick look.

Joshua, indicating the tarp, mouthed to Bjorn, "Which one is under there?"

Bjorn mouthed back the word, "ring". But Joshua didn't understand.

Bjorn spoke clearly, "String!"

The tiny woman tapped her baton against a nearby chair, and said to the members of her group, "Ladies, we've been asked to sing. Vim and vigor, Ladies!"

All stopped what they were doing and burst into song under the direction of their choir mistress, and had a jolly time rendering a classic a-cappella hymnal.

After they were done, everyone clapped and the ladies shyly curtsied.

Noah still clapping asked Bjorn, "And what was the fate of the attorney?"

Bjorn replied, "Atsushi could have shot me, an ordinary reporter, right in the face and gotten away with it, but he made the mistake of attacking a high-level corporate executive, which was like attacking the whole corporate hierarchy itself."

Sarah clarified, "Attorney Atsushi killed Skipper Courtly..."

The group sitting around them gave a little gasp, but remained silent.

"And," Sarah continued, not realizing the effect of her comments on the nearby listeners, "He attempted to also kill Pip. Atsushi will definitely be in prison forever."

Her listeners quietly glanced at each other, eyes wide.

"For now, at least," Bjorn added sardonically.

Alexandra asked, "So, cousin Pip is on the mend? Won't he want to regain control of the Courtly companies?"

"No, I don't think so," Bjorn shared. "That's my opinion, but he did agree to accept retirement, so..."

Joshua piped in, "Retirement? Isn't Pip too young to retire..."

Bjorn laughed, "Pip Courtly is going to get as much money as any of those over-paid executives get when they retire; a huge allowance for life in exchange for not being imprisoned as an accomplice to Atsushi. Pip also formally relinquished all managerial control of Courtly holdings."

Noah suggested, "I suppose that is good enough, as long as that fellow remembers Proverbs sixteen says, 'How much better it is to have wisdom and good judgment than gold'."

"So," Ruth Lantz asked, "Will Pip be pursing his glass blowing artwork, then?"

"Probably," Sarah replied, "But he can do whatever he likes after he completes his rehab treatments. He mentioned he'd like to open a gallery to show off his glass art."

Then Joshua, unable to hold back any longer, interrupted, "Everyone. Please."

The entire crowd turned toward him.

"I asked you all here," Joshua spoke with a nervous tremble in his voice, "to congratulate Alexandra on becoming the new Liaison from our village to Courtly Dynamics Corporation."

The entire room went quiet, then broke into happy applause. Alexandra blushed.

"And," Joshua continued, "I know that Alexandra will represent our village well. And the dumping of polluted waste will permanently stop."

The tiny enthusiastic group applauded again, and broke into excited chatter.

Joshua now walked over to the wood working alcove and lifted up a corner of the tarp, holding it in his hand.

"And," Joshua continued, "I also want

to acknowledge that I respect the culture Alexandra came from as she has always respected ours."

Again, the gathering applauded cheerfully.

Bjorn leaned over to Sarah and lowered his voice. "Watch. This will be a great follow up story for Sammy's new Investigative Reporting Division..."

"At the Daily Memo?" Sarah asked. Bjorn's wink confirmed her question as she happily squeezed his good arm, then turned to pay full attention to Joshua and Alexandra.

Abruptly, Joshua whipped back the canvas tarp with his eyes closed, trembling.

The audience gasped.

"Oh, that is so cute," Alexandra said as she picked up the jar and opened it. She inhaled deeply, "Thank you Joshua. I've always liked Mama's soaps."

Bjorn blanched.

Joshua looked at Bjorn bewildered, "Wasn't it: the bar is in the jar?"

Sarah got up and while the group was ooh-ing and ah-ing over the soap that Joshua had just given to Alexandra, Sarah took the opportunity to step into the kitchen, but couldn't remember if her gift to Bjorn was by the cask or on the other end of the counter behind the flask...

She quickly stepped over to the flask and picked it up, but didn't see the gift wrapped box she wanted to give to Bjorn. It wasn't anywhere near the cask, either.

She caught Alexandra's eye, but Alexandra shrugged, timidly indicating she didn't know where it had gone.

As Sarah looked around, she saw that Noah Lantz had taken a drink from the flask, found the box she intended for Bjorn, and apparently thought it must be a surprise gift from his wife to him. He was looking at the box adoringly as he approached Ruth, smiling, to thank her.

Ruth shook her head, confused.

Joshua looked at Bjorn with pleading eyes.

Bjorn tried to remember where he had put it.

Joshua recited softly himself, "the star with the tar. No. The Czar was too far. No..." He stood awkwardly as one of the ladies started to speak with Bjorn.

The woman looked at Bjorn's injury and said, "Oh, that must be awkward to walk on- that crutch."

Joshua, still reciting, muttered, "The crutch in the hutch. No the Dutch asked how much? Um."

Bjorn leaned over to Joshua, "Where is the box? Did you move it?"

Bjorn knew where he had placed the box, but Joshua must have moved it because it was no longer where Bjorn hid it earlier.

Joshua spoke with frozen lips through his teeth to Bjorn, "Right, I saw you put it down and knew it was too obvious, so I moved it."

Noah asked, "I can't remember when the last time I had carp. Ruthie, what did we have last Sunday at your mother's?"

"It was slow cooked and very tender Ox," Ruth replied to her husband.

Joshua muttered, "The box is by the ox that squawks?"

"On a string?" Bjorn prompted trying to help.

On hearing the word "string," the ladies in the room burst into song again, quite distracting Joshua.

"The box with the blocks has the ring on a string!" Joshua was pleased with himself as he remembered.

The ladies enthusiastically sang another melody.

Bjorn turned to Joshua, "I hid it on the side table near the sofa. Where did you move it to?"

Joshua mentally reviewed his actions in his head. He thought. Then remembering, whispered to Bjorn, "I put it in a drawer near the door."

Bjorn congratulated him, "Good. You don't need to rhyme anymore. Go get it."

Joshua hurried to the china hutch, opened the cabinet door, then pulled open a drawer inside, produced the box, and smiled triumphantly at Bjorn.

Sarah tapped Ruth on the shoulder, but by then Noah had already opened up the box he had taken from the kitchen. He saw the harp paperweight and was very perplexed by it. His wife Ruth was still confused as to where the box came from.

"Oh, I'm so sorry," Sarah said, "but I was going to surprise Bjorn with that…"

"Of course," Noah chortled, "You realize we don't play musical instruments in our village," he smiled understandingly as he mended the slightly ripped wrapping paper, and handed it to Sarah.

"It appears to be a day of gift mix-ups," Ruth started, "Miss Paradise, I made this especially for you. I'm not sure why Joshua gave it to Alexandra." She handed Sarah the scented soaps. Sarah opened the jar, and inhaled the strong floral fragrance.

"Thank you so much. It's truly heavenly! I really do appreciate your thoughtfulness, Mrs. Lantz."

Then, Sarah headed straight to Bjorn before anything else could happen.

Joshua, catching Alexandra by surprise, took her by one hand.

Bjorn used his crutch, struggled to his feet, and waved his good arm, "Everyone. Please direct your attention to Mr. Joshua Lantz. Over here." Then Bjorn, sat down, to give the "stage" to Joshua.

Everyone stopped talking and turned toward Joshua and Alexandra.

Joshua, dropping down on one knee, as Bjorn had coached him earlier, looked earnestly up at Alexandra, who was very confused as to what was going on.

"Did you lose something Joshua?"

Alexandra asked.

"Only my heart... to you..." He presented her with the box he had finally retrieved.

She opened it, staring. It was a small, sparkling ring.

"Will you marry me, Alexandra?"

"Oh! Joshua," she replied, unable to stop smiling, "Yes!"

"And papa said that he can walk you down the aisle since your father is in heaven," Joshua added.

"You knew about this?" Sarah asked Mr. Lantz.

Noah Lantz smiled, "We are good at keeping secrets when needed."

Everyone clustered excitedly around the newly engaged couple. The ladies were especially curious as to why Joshua had given a ring to Alexandra, since in their community they don't exchange rings. The men asked him why Joshua had knelt on one knee.

Joshua, taking command, explained the engagement customs he had learned from Bjorn about the culture Alexandra came from.

Off on the sofa, Sarah snuggled up next to Bjorn.

"Was that your surprise for me?" Sarah asked. "Their engagement? How wonderful."

"I kept it secret for a month," Bjorn boasted playfully. "And weren't you surprised?"

"Definitely," Sarah grinned. "Here is my surprise to you." And she presented him with the slightly torn box.

"You were my guardian angel that night. You saved my life. Thank you."

"This is great!" Bjorn smiled as he held the little harp paperweight in his hand, "And I thought I could read all your secrets. I really wasn't expecting this."

Bjorn gently wrapped one hand around Sarah's and held on.

"I'm not quite done, Bjorn," Sarah teased.

"With what?" he asked

"With my surprises." Sarah got up and looked out the window. The sun was beginning to set.

Bjorn hobbled over on his crutch and asked, "Want to leave already?"

"No, Bjorn. Just looking at the beautiful horizon."

She leaned against him, "I guess you knew Joshua was going to propose, didn't you?"

"Yup. Men always know before the women," he smiled.

Then Sarah turned toward Bjorn and said, "Let's join the party."

The entire group now wandered into the dining room, an extension of the large kitchen, where the table was covered with an array of tasty foods. Noah Lantz helped situate Bjorn in his own chair while Ruth filled Bjorn's plate with goodies.

Sarah slipped away from the crowd and, unnoticed, walked out the front door.

On the porch, she met the approaching Detective Gene striding down the path toward the house.

"Did you tell anybody?" Gene asked Sarah.

"Not a word. Did you tell them?" Sarah asked.

"No," Gene smiled, "I said I had to stop off at a friend's first and just invited them in. Here they come. It's been a long journey."

"I think you can tell them, now. It's time. The front door is unlocked. Come in when you are ready. We are around the corncr to the left in the dining room." Sarah smiled and ran back inside.

Sarah returned to the little party. Most never noticed she had left.

A few moments later, the voice said, "Where's my Ace?"

Alexandra stood bolt upright, frozen, and unsure.

Everyone fell silent.

Then, from around the corner emerged Mr. Jack Courtly and his wife, Queenie. They both inhaled sharply as they immediately recognized Alexandra, their daughter.

Words stuck in Alexandra's throat. She was unable to move, unable to react.

How could this be? What was she seeing? Was it her imagination?

She stepped slowly, unbelieving, out into the living room, where her parents stood, and the rest of the group followed.

Queenie, wearing simple garb, broke the silence by stepping toward her daughter, saying, "My precious baby Ace. I told you we'd come for you when we could. Believe me, this is the first chance that your Daddy and I could."

Both Jack and Queenie, unprepared for the impact of this moment, felt hot salty tears well up in their eyes.

Queenie stood, with her hands covering her mouth, uncertain that she was really seeing her only child.

"She's so tall, now," Jack whispered.

Forcing herself to take a breath, her lips unable to form words, Alexandra cautiously stumbled toward this apparition, her mother and father, whom she had thought were dead.

Queenie embraced her tightly, afraid to breathe.

"Thank you, Ruth," Queenie choked out as tears streamed down her cheeks, "for keeping your word and taking care of my baby for me 'til I could come for her."

Ruth Lantz was speechless. Noah slowly got to his feet.

Sarah seemed to be the only one able to talk, and she spoke softly to Mr. and Mrs. Courtly. "They call her Alexandra, now, instead of Ace."

Sarah helped Bjorn stand up and he instinctively put a loving arm around her.

Queenie smiled, closing her eyes as she embraced the daughter she hadn't seen in so very long.

"Seven years," Queenie gasped. "The Lantz's watched you for seven years. Oh, Ruth. Thank you so much. How was it? I can't imagine!"

Ruth offered, "It was a little rough at first, but she matured quickly. Developed good habits of working hard."

Then, Ruth remembered something.

"Oh, Alexandra," Ruth turned toward the girl she had learned to love like a daughter, "I think this would be the right time, don't you?"

Alexandra nodded, understanding, broke free of her mother's embrace and stepped away quickly, gesturing she would be right back.

Bjorn hobbled forward on one crutch when, in the shadows, he saw a familiar form.

"Detective Gene?" Bjorn asked squinting.

Sarah interjected, "At the station, it was Detective Gene who worked with me to figure out where Alexandra's parents were located."

Detective Gene smiled as he stepped into the light.

The guests gasped simultaneously when they saw the SP. Then, they broke into hurried whispers to each other as they tried to figure out the back story which led to what was transpiring before them.

Alexandra returned holding a package with both arms. It was wrapped in plain paper and twine. The top was a little dusty.

Ruth coaxed Alexandra to speak.

"I... I...," was all Alexandra could say as she held the package.

Ruth helped her out and turned toward the Courtlys, "Your little Ace wants to give you this."

Ruth indicated that Alexandra should hand the package over.

She did.

Queenie and Jack accepted it. They both opened it.

After tentatively pulling away the edge of the paper, they saw it was a corner of a quilt. A rather large quilt. Queenie looked at it, speechless.

Ruth continued, "It's the pattern you designed, Mrs. Courtly, remember? For your vacation cottage? For Alexandra's, oh I mean, Ace's room?"

"Yes. Of course!" Queenie whispered hoarsely.

"Your own very dear daughter created this quilt with her very own hand. Poor thing." Ruth put an arm around Alexandra, "She missed you both so terribly. She shed a tear for each stitch connecting the edges. She quilted the finest cottons we could find."

Noah added, "My Ruthie kept encouraging Alexandra, keeping her hope alive, assuring her that you'd come for her if God allowed for it. Now you see your pattern is more beautiful when sewn by your daughter's hand."

Alexandra, tears pouring down her face, rushed to Queenie and Jack hugging them both fiercely.

"Yes, Mommy and Daddy, please accept this gift. I'll bet you never expected me to appreciate hand crafts... especially the art of quilting!"

Alexandra laughed through her tears.

Jack took the quilt and flung it out, so it unfurled and drifted softly on top of the sofa for everyone to see. Queenie and Jack invited Bjorn and Sarah to examine it closely. The detailed handiwork was breathtaking.

Jack said, "Baby Ace, it's beautiful. Just beautiful." His voice cracked as his trembling hand touched the treasure his daughter had created.

Queenie reached into her handbag and pulled out two tattered quilt squares with bullet holes and faded bloodstains, both now freshly stitched together.

It was the same pattern.

It was what had silently connected them all these years. Each Courtly was a separate scrap of fabric, meaningless and alone. Only finding their beauty when the family was stitched together again into a stunning quilt which could provide comfort and warmth to those it surrounded.

Bjorn and Sarah withdrew a bit to give the family time to reunite. Queenie hugged Ruth.

Noah Lantz clasped Jack Courtly's hand as he spoke gratefully, "I never thanked you for saving my life on the train. For taking my place all these years." Jack nodded in silence, and shook Noah's hand firmly.

Detective Gene stepped toward Jack, "Mr. Courtly, if you had not intervened during the prison break years ago, I would not be alive today. Thank you."

Jack replied as he placed his hand on the SP's shoulder, "You already thanked me when you picked me up, a crippled man, on that empty road, and brought me to the Rest Haven Inn, where I found my wife. And you found us again to bring our family together."

"And Miss Paradise," Alexandra said, "I never thanked you for taking my place when you were accused of stealing that secret file, which proved my uncle and Atsushi were frauds. You endured life-threatening punishments meant for me."

She ran and hugged Sarah.

Noah turned and made an announcement to all the guests in his living room. "We are thankful to have friends like Mr. Esterday, Miss Paradise, and Mr. Gene who had the patience to piece all the clues together. God granted them unique opportunities and wisdom to find you, Mr. and Mrs. Courtly, and bring you home..."

"And have the courts," Jack stated triumphantly, "declare me legally alive. I know I have some messes to clean up... and we will..."

They had nearly forgotten about him,

but now Joshua Lantz stood up and approached Jack Courtly.

"Sir," Joshua started, swallowing hard, "this may be a terrible time, but please forgive me and assume I am too young to know any better."

Jack turned toward the young man.

"I remember you from the train, Joshua." Jack smiled, "I'll bet you've been Ace's friend and confidant all these years." He extended his hand to Joshua.

Joshua nervously wiped his now clammy hands on his pant legs and, trembling, accepted Jack's proffered hand. He stumbled over his words, "Mr. Courtly, I mean, could I. I mean, I'd like permission for Lexi. I mean Alexandra, I mean Ace. Sir? Would you mind if I married your daughter?"

Jack and Queenie stunned, with their mouths opened, didn't know what to think, turning to each other to see who would react first. Alexandra's face blushed red. Joshua marched directly to Alexandra and grabbed her hand firmly.

Joshua looked Jack straight in the eye, fighting off fear. Alexandra's eyes were downcast as she extended her hand to show her father the ring Joshua had just given her.

"Nice ring," Jack smiled, but his voice broke

The lady with the baton rapped the nearby table and the a-cappella choir burst into harmoniously joyful song, accompanied by the enthusiastic applause of the guests.

4 CHAPTER Year 2037: AnCors Away (Continuous Ch 88)

"What is that, Percy?" Slash asked, as he sat down in a new campsite, carefully hidden deep in the forest. Not many AnCors were there, but Slash wanted to hear Percy's plans. Plans needed funding.

Percy, hair cleaned, wore the suit Jack Courtly had been captured in seven years earlier. The jacket arms and pant legs were cuffed to fit Percy. He took good care of those clothes and wore them when he wanted to seduce potential clients into supporting his anti-corporatism ideals.

He opened the box he had just received from a recent sponsor in town, so Slash and the others could see the latest technology in weaponry.

"Is that from our new client?" Slash asked.

"Another corporate king. Wants two other cities to fight against each other," Percy stated plainly, "Our numbers have thinned, but our new sponsor's funding will fortify our defenses against the SPs, get us new recruits, build up this campsite-and more."

"So... we're starting a war between two corporations who trade with each other?" Slash asked.

"Our client makes weapons. He needs customers. He's hiring us to pit two neighboring corporate cities against each other. Start a war so he has customers for his goods," Percy explained.

"The money will get us back to where we were, right? It'll be enough to teach our old thorns a thing or two, won't it?" Slash asked.

"Yeah. None of us has to like that these monarchs have so much, just that they will give it to me," Percy closed the box.

He carefully removed the clothes he had worn at his meeting with the corporation liaison, while the other AnCors gathered sticks to make a small fire.

Percy packed away Jack's old suit and replaced it by donning his usual uniform of worn, ripe, shabby garb. Now, city folk would faint at his overpowering stench, but he was more comfortable this way.

Percy walked around the small campfire, where the others began to seat themselves. He waited a moment as the sticks crackled in the flames and sparks evaporated skyward into the setting sun.

Then, Percy eased himself down onto a nearby boulder and murmured,

"Evil kings and lords rule, then depart.

Self-loving royals mount new corporate thrones.

Such monarchs boast they'll reign with

good intent.

Yet, still they will not see the shining truth.

That we, the people, want no kings at all."

"No kings!" Slash and the others echoed in unison, "We'll have no kings at all...!"

The sun dipped below the horizon of the squalid camp and unfolded a blanket of rich ebony sky. Then, the first star of night appeared.

☆ **THE END** ☆

Or is it?

5 CHAPTER- Postword

Later in 2036, at the Soldier Police Prison, Atsushi is incarcerated. "Life without parole". Of course, perhaps the cleanliness standards of the prison cause Atsushi's lip to snarl in disgust, but this is the life he clearly selects for himself based on the choices he prefers to make on his own broken moral compass.

Pip Courtly, however, is back to blowing glass trinkets in his home... with his own set of friends.

At what was once Skipper Courtly's private lake, the Widow's Cloister's Eldress is directing the sisters and widows to move their cloistered living to Skipper's old residence, his castle. Some of the more mechanically inclined sisters are working on the basement, by collaborating with the construction crews to make it water tight. Skipper had once called it his dungeon. All the artifacts are being brought up one story to create a museum of sorts.

The sisters are using their best calligraphy skills to pen Bible verses to warn others about the lust for power for power's sake and instead to rely on God as well as how to recognize the fruits of the spirit.

The Monastery Brothers are helping to convert the Throne room into a chapel and moving some of the heavier Holy Relics and artifacts into place to set up a welcoming environment for parishioners.

Mrs. Queenie Courtly, without her finery, is helping in the move.

Meanwhile, in the Earth Farmer fields, the Courtly trucks are sanitizing the dirt, removing any trace from Mayfounder pollution to allow the environment and soil to be tilled by the Earth Farmers to produce healthy food.

The Elders of the Earth Farmers community finally feel as if the Courtly Family is working on their behalf so they can plant and harvest wholesome nourishments to sell to the citizens of Courtly City. As we all know, the varieties the Earth Farmers grow, are the most delicious and nutritious.

Sarah Paradise returns to teaching her students, who all seem to enjoy learning. As the students are dismissed from class, Bjorn Esterday enters Sarah's classroom against the flow of departing students. Gingerly, he helps scoop up Sarah's belongings and carries them out, assisting Sarah graciously. He then drives off with Sarah, both smiling.

Alexandra Lantz works with her mother-in-law Ruth to stitch together the final edges of a new quilt with precise deft needle and thread, just as the old masters used to do.

6 CHAPTER Did You Know?

Celery

Cultural Note about the EARTH FARMERS: Celery is an important part of the Earth Farmer wedding ceremony as it's used for stuffing fowl, and as appetizers served during large village banquets.

When a family plants extra celery, it is a clue that somebody in the household will soon marry. Earth Farmer weddings do not take a lot of planning. Weddings require about two or three weeks of preparation. Those not baptized in the Earth Farmer faith can marry outside the faith and not be "shunned".

Most Earth Farmer weddings are in November or December after the harvest. If a villager marries a person who is also "in the faith", the bride's wedding dress is new and blue. The ceremony and reception is at the bride's house. If a villager marries outside the faith, the bride will wear a simple white dress and will marry in a church with music, but some traditional relatives may disapprove of this and not attend because the bride's dress is white and not blue. Both versions of the wedding prevent shunning of the young couple, and the couple is welcomed into the community.

Biurnal tides

The fictional term "biurnal", referenced in this story, doubles the two 12-hour Diurnal cycles. That means the fictional "biurnal" low-tide cycle is 24 hours, and the "biurnal" high tide cycle is also 24 hours making the entire "biurnal" cycle 48 hours. That, of course, is twice the time of a genuine scientifically-proven Diurnal cycle.

Diurnal tides have a period of approximately 24 hours (1 day),

The Bay of Fundy (French: *Baie de Fundy*): Fundy bay has the biggest difference between tide levels, (about 50 feet high at high tide). The Gulf of Mexico, has only one high and one low tide each lunar day. This is called a diurnal tide. The U.S. West Coast tends to have mixed semidiurnal tides, whereas a semidiurnal pattern is more typical of the East Coast (*Sumich, J.L., 1996; Thurman, H.V., 1994; Ross, D.A., 1995*).

A lunar day is measured as the time between two successive crossings of the moon over the earth's Prime Meridian, about 24 hours and 50 minutes.

EDGES Reference to Biurnal Tides

After Bjorn's eyes adjusted, he couldn't

believe what he saw. Just the day before, the basement had been a place designated for simple storage. Now it looked as if a giant hand had tossed about all the chess pieces on a board, leaving exactly one large item, the coffin, propped upright. The difference was that these were not simple little game pieces. These were massive wooden statues, very old and damaged from being rattled about so frequently. But, consistently, that coffin always wound up standing on its end.

EXCERPT from **Book 5 , 1 CHAPTER Year Year 2036: Castle Dungeon (Continuous Ch 43)**

Dim flickering lights barely illuminated the center of the room. Bjorn's eyes were adjusting from the bright day outside to this poorly lit interior, and now he saw what was before him.

Skipper looked at Bjorn for a reaction, "You see it?"

Bjorn nodded. All the objects, which he remembered being neatly arranged along one wall, were now wildly tossed about into a scrambled heap. Standing in the midst of the haphazard jumble of carved wooden statuary, a large coffin loomed upright on one end.

"Sure is a mess," Bjorn stated simply.

Later …

EXCERPT from **Book 8, Chapter 2, Consecutive Chapter 76- Year 2036: Celery**

"Oh, he (Bjorn) told me. It was because the lady at the florist was explaining how to calculate volume for a small pond. Then, he remembered the boat in the Castle lake. He figured out that the tides of that lake come in every other day. Rare biurnal tides rush in fast and pull out faster than a regular tide. So, every other day, lake water would seep into the basement, flooding it up to the ceiling, making it appear that the coffin was emanating powers to toss the statues around."

"I saw that coffin when I was down there," Sarah interjected. "I'll bet the *heavy ornate iron work at the base weighed it down so that it was the only object that didn't float around."*

Alexandra nodded, "No ghost. Just physics. God even used mundane circumstances to bring Bjorn to you in time, Miss Paradise."

Breaking glass

So, for a diva to successfully demolish the wine glass with her voice, she would have to fortuitously choose a crystal with sufficient microscopic defects that would allow the crystal to shatter from the vibrations of sympathetic frequency.

Invisible cracks and chinks cover every material's surface, but their size and location can vary wildly, according to Kysar. Wine glasses, which appear to be identical to the naked eye, could have radically different fracture strengths, enabling some to withstand much higher levels of vocal volume than others.

Volume is a key player in the glass shattering game, because the loudness of a sound is directly related to the extent it displaces air molecules. In essence, the sound passes from molecule to molecule until it hits the glass. As Brunhilde sings louder, she is increasing the speed and pressure of air being pushed at the glass. The effect is much like pushing a kid on a swing—the harder each shove becomes, the sooner the kid will go over the top.

But one strong shove has little effect unless it is timed so it matches the natural oscillation of the swing—just as a hopeful vocal glass-breaker must sing a note that truly matches the resonant frequency of the glass.

Only the finest lead-crystal is fragile and resonant enough to break at volumes that some singers can produce without amplification—upward of 100 decibels.

In 2005, the Discovery Channel television show 'Myth Busters' tackled this question, recruiting rock singer and vocal coach Jamie Vendera to hit some crystal-ware with his best vocal sound.

He tried 12 different wine glasses before stumbling on the lucky one that splintered at the blast of his mighty pipes. For the first time, proof that an unassisted voice can indeed shatter glass was captured on video.

Vendera's glass-breaking wail registered at 105 decibels—almost as loud as a jackhammer. Not many people can muster the lung power for that kind of noise. Opera singers train for years to build up the strength to produce sustained notes at volumes above 100 decibels. (By comparison, typical speech is around 50 decibels.)

Hot Air Balloons

In 1989, one balloon crash killed 13 people in Australia when two hot air balloons collided.

If fuel runs out, the balloon will simply float down like a parachute, which means it is possible to land safely

81% of crashes happen during attempts to land.

65% involve crash landing to the ground.

Researchers from the national safety board, studied 10 years of balloon flights. They found that 618 people had serious injuries or died from balloon crashes.

Broken legs and broken ankles make up about 50% of the injuries reported during the study period.

Other crashes can occur mid-air, but may involve crashing into trees, buildings, or powerlines.

When these sorts of crashes occur, the basket – or gondola- is dragged, tipped, or bounced. All of these options can throw the occupants out onto the ground, sometimes killing them.

In addition to hot air balloon crashes, fires are also a threat to balloon travel.

What could cause a fire during a balloon ride?

Fires can happen when the balloon hits power lines, or something goes wrong with the flames heating the balloon. Sometimes, too many people cram into the balloon basket, which could cause the balloon to move irregularly.

So, you need to make sure your balloon pilots are skilled and know what they are doing.

In 1783, Pilltre De Rozier launched the first hot air balloon, holding a sheep, a duck and a rooster. The balloon stayed aloft for 15 minutes.

In 1784, Vincent Lunardi flew a hydrogen balloon over London. He flew 13 miles, which lasted about an hour and a half.

Joseph Mont Golfier flew the largest man-carrying balloon, which could hold about 30 people.

In 1785, an American (John Jefferies) and a French man (Jean Blanchard) crossed the English channel in a balloon. They carried a letter, which made this the first air mail delivery.

1797 witnessed the first parachute jump from a balloon. It was made by a French Balloonist named "Garnerin".

Many hot-air balloon pilots thought if they went too high, they'd be electrocuted by clouds. James Glaisher and Henry Coxwell decided to find out for themselves. In 1862, they went up 7 miles or 39,000 feet, heading toward the stratosphere.

They didn't realize that they were losing oxygen by heading so high. Mr. Glaisher was busy measuring air pressure, temperature, and speed as the air was thinning during the balloon ascent. He lost consciousness and collapsed because of the thinning oxygen.

Fortunately, his partner in the basket, Coxwell was getting light headed and grew weak. It was about 12F. Very cold. He forced the cord that regulated air pressure into his teeth and tried to release air pressure so the balloon would drop slowly.

Before Coxwell passed out, Glaisher began to revive as the balloon lowered to the earth. Their oxygen supply increased as winds whipped around their tiny basket.

They eventually landed safely with an immense amount of information. In particular, they learned about the need to deal with reduced oxygen and decreased air pressure at those heights.

1876 the British formed the British Balloon Corps. Balloons began to be used in the military.

In 1900, Gorden Bennett, an American News reporter, actually sponsored the first balloon race from Paris. They still hold this balloon race regularly.

In 1932, the first balloon flight to reach the stratosphere (that is 52,498 feet) was sent up by August Piccard.

In 1935, a gas balloon was sent up 72,000 feet, which is about 13 miles. Two crew members rode in a pressurized chamber. It was the first to carry live radio broadcasts.

In 1960, American air force captain, Joe Kittinger, jumped from a balloon almost 103,000 feet in the air with nothing but a parachute. He broke the sound barrier with his body.

Hot Air Ballooning was not officially a sport until the 1970's. (1963 was the first U. S. National Hot Air Balloon Championship event held in Kalamazoo, Michigan.) They used synthetic material for the fabric instead of silk. Manufacturing took place in the United Kingdom. Small burners were added to provide a constant flame needed to generate the hot air for balloon lift.

In 1978, the first balloon crossed the Atlantic ocean. It was called the Double Eagle 2.

In 1981, the Double Eagle 5 was the first balloon to cross the Pacific Ocean, travelling from Japan to California USA. (Ben Abruzzo, Larry Newman, Ron Clark and Rocky Aoki).

Although the classic story "Around the World in 80 Days" is about a global hot air ballooning adventure, the first historically successful balloon ride around the world in real life took place in 1999. It took 20 days.

Air ballooning was the first time man actually felt as if he flew.

Paper Weight

Proverbs 11:28 "Those who trust in their riches will fall like dead leaves, but good people will blossom".

In an earlier chapter, Sarah bought Bjorn a paperweight to thank him for saving her life.

Why did she select a paperweight in a high-tech world? Sarah respects Bjorn's old fashioned morals and manners. So, Sarah wanted to use a gift (that was traditionally given to nobility) to thank him. Thus, the paperweight.

The function of a paperweight is fairly basic. It was a weight to place on top of your paper records to keep them from blowing away or off a desk.

What materials were paperweights first made of?
The famous ones were created in glass or crystal.

Glass paperweights began to be manufactured in France in 1845 by such glass factories as Baccarat, St. Louis, and Clichy in an effort to create expensive luxury items. Other companies got into the game around 1851 during the Great Exhibition of London

These fancy paperweights were developed as elegant gift items for kings and nobility.

Three French companies made them primarily for royalty and the wealthy upper class. When did other glass makers get into the game of making and selling paperweights?

In 1851 paperweights were shown off at the Great Exhibition of London. Other factories joined in to create grand presentation pieces with intricate designs.

How long were paperweights popular?

They were popular back then, and even more today. Back in the 1950's, fancy paper weights became all the rage when Paul Jokelson encouraged French glass factories to re-invent the technique.

This way, modern paperweights were brighter and more complex than the originals.

Many paperweights are on display in famous museums and private collections.

Paperweights were an expensive collectors item. They cost a lot to acquire, but they were easy to maintain. They required no special temperature or humidity settings as do other collections, such as oil paintings or stamps. This is why paperweights were considered very desirable to collect.

There are several types of paperweights:

Mille Fiori are thousands of tiny glass flowers inside the paperweight.

Lamp caught real flowers and butterflies.

Sulfide embeds 3-D miniatures.

Swirl colors radiating like pinwheels.

Victorian shows pictures of people in milk glass.

Californian where the surface melts glass bits, then is sprayed with hot metallic sparkling salts.

What does a Millie Fiori look like?

Mille Fiori: They look like hundreds of flowers caught in crystal. They are actually made from tubes of colored glass rods and exist in many variations.

How would a Lamp work paperweight differ from the Mille Fiori?

Lamp work: These contain real flower petals and butterflies along with other beautiful samples of nature.

Sulfide paperweights: these have 3-D miniatures made from ceramics embedded inside the glass. They are used to commemorate a person or event.

Swirl paperweights: these have two or three colors radiating like a pin wheel caught in crystal.

Another paperweight style is named after a state: the **Californian**. Californian paperweight: These are made by painting the surface of the dome with colored pieces of melting glass which are shaped by picks and tools. They are then sprayed with hot metallic salt to achieve a sparkling look.

Victorian portrait paperweight: This is a glass dome first made in Pennsylvania. It contains pictures of ordinary people reproduced with milk-glass and encased in clear glass.

The factors influencing the value of a paperweight are: Design, how Rare it is, the Condition it is in, and the Workmanship.

Designers must avoid bubbles, and yellow or green cast to the glass.

In stamp collecting, upside down pictures can make the item more valuable, but in paperweights mistakes are not tolerated.

What are some other things a collector should avoid. Bad things to look out for in a paperweight?

As noted earlier, bubbles can affect the value, and good collections do not accept glass that has a yellow or green cast. These good collections also reject uneven spacing or broken elements.

There are no unintended accidents that will be accepted in an expensive paperweight. In stamps, by contrast, if the image is accidentally printed upside down, this can add to its value. Not so with paperweights. Everything must be executed as planned by the artist.

Baccarat glass in France was one of the best houses to make glass paperweights. Baccarat needed trees for special fuel to keep the glass molten as it was formed. They needed clean sand for the glass itself. They needed access to various minerals for experimentation with color.

The Baccarat glass factory was not always owned by the French. It was taken over by Germany in the Franco Prussian war of 1871. It went back to France at the end of WWI in 1918. It was taken over by Germany again in WWII from 1940-44.

Then, it was returned to France, where it is still owned by France to this very day.

7 CHAPTER- What Will Happen Next?

Earth Farmers would quote the Biblical reference of Romans 8:28, *"And we know that for those who love God all things work together for good, for those who are called according to his purpose."*

So, how did all things work out in EDGES? Did *"all things work together for good..."*?

Jack Courtly endured difficult situations, but his reactions demonstrated he made ethical choices in response to the adversity. At first, it may have seemed that he was not making progress, but in the end, it all came together to benefit not just Jack, but many other people who also operated with good intentions, and were happily impacted by Jack's choices.

Jack and Queenie become more thoughtful, patient, wise leaders, focused on what is good and true. Both of the Courtly's also show genuine appreciation for the efforts Earth Farmer Noah and Ruth Lantz made to secretly raise Ace during a turbulent and uncertain time in Courtly City. The Lantz family, after all, did not know if Jack and Queenie were dead or alive. During the frustratingly slow process of trying to find each other, Jack and Queenie re-prioritize what is important and eventually are reunited with their child, Ace.

Ace may have initially been self-absorbed and shallow, seeking only what is entertaining, but adversity taught Ace to have an inquiring mind, as well as to hone instincts into talents which would help an entire community. Activities, such as the tedious discipline needed to hand stitch the edges of a quilt together, were initially mocked by Ace, but now the reader can discern the appreciation of effort such detailed work takes to contribute to a beautiful heirloom quilt. Ace takes that newfound appreciation, then combines it with her Courtly leadership skills and becomes the liason to get the Earth Farmer village-farmed food into Courtly City for distribution so that all citizens can benefit from fresh wholesome produce grown the old fashioned way.

Pip himself will focus on his passion of glass blowing. After seeing that ruthless unbridled ambition cost Pip's father, Skipper Courtly, his life, Pip has learned the benefit of helping his family to build instead of trying to undermine and divide in order to better control the citizens Courtly City. Pip will support the original ruling family, Jack and Queenie and Ace Courtly, take back control of Courtly City.

Everyone expresses gratitude for the seemingly insignificant part each person played, which culminated into a beautifully woven intricate plot, resulting in the unlikely reunion of a family and the "righting" of many wrongs.

But jealously looms ominously in the background as the AnCors, Percy Snatcher and Slash with their followers, have gotten a new source of funding to start another corporate-city war... and they end in iambic pentameter. Ironically, Percy speaks so angrily about having kings rule these corporate cities, but he himself has made himself a king of the AnCors. He is a brutal dictator removing those who cause him inconvenience without thought to long-term consequences or group morale. Where will Percy's choices lead all the AnCors who look to him for direction?

EDGES reveals how Sarah Paradise meets Bjorn Esterday. Both of them discover that they share a solid moral compass. They do what is right, even if, at first, it means they face difficult consequences. But, in the long run, will doing the right thing pay off in the end?

Suddenly, Bjorn Esterday vanishes!

Sarah can't find out where he's GONE. Or why. One day he pops back into her life! Will she ever discover what happened to Bjorn Esterday during his astonishing absence from Courtly City?

ം The End ൦

ABOUT Wynter Sommers

Wynter Sommers is the pseudonym for an American writing team, which harnesses multiple skills in technology, research, and education. Formally trained with a PhD in Education, Wynter Sommers blends academic classroom experience, with corporate sophistication, and a passion for developing more effective student insights.

Wynter Sommers has taught classrooms of enthusiastic children. She has a heart to inspire creativity and develop critical thinking skills, all to encourage students to make wise choices in life. She wants to impart the talent of honing one's skills in self-reliance and collaborative team work. Despite any environmental barriers outside of an individual's control, Wynter Sommers wishes to impart the message that genuine hope, love, and peace can help us overcome obstacles, and cement friendships. Wynter Sommers hopes you enjoy the other *Bjorn Esterday Was not Born Yesterday* stories in this series.

www.ingramcontent.com/pod-product-compliance
Lightning Source LLC
Chambersburg PA
CBHW051841020726
47502CB00005B/1899